5497

11067194 1

976
.20

Texas Rose

Rita Kerr

EAKIN PRESS ☆ Austin, Texas

Stories For Young Americans Series

FIRST EDITION

Copyright © 1986
By Rita Kerr

Published in the United States of America
By Eakin Press, P.O. Box 23069, Austin, Texas 78735

ISBN 0-89015-578-X

Library of Congress Cataloging-in-Publication Data

Kerr, Rita.
    Texas Rose.

    Summary: Recounts the experiences of eight-year-old Dilue and her family who came to settle in Texas during its struggle to break from Mexico.
    1. Harris, Rose Dilue, 1825–1914 — Juvenile fiction. 2. Texas — History — to 1846 — Juvenile fiction.
    [1. Harris, Rose Dilue, 1825–1914 — Fiction. 2. Texas — History — to 1846 — Fiction. 3. Frontier and pioneer life — Fiction] I. Title.
PZ7.K468458Te   1986   [Fic]   86-16648
ISBN 0-89015-578-X

*This book is dedicated
to the author's grandsons,*

Larry and Jimmy Kerr

Contents

Acknowledgments

The author finds it difficult to express her gratitude to all who influenced the writing of *Texas Rose,* but special thanks goes to the librarians of the Daughters of the Republic of Texas Library at the Alamo. Sincere thanks goes to these librarians for their interest in this book: Nancy Hughes, Lavern Wilson, Pat Haby, Eloise Mabrita and friends, Dr. Amy Jo Baker, and B. Sharp. A word of appreciation goes to the author's mother, Maya Wilson; her children, Kay Stephens and Don Kerr; and grandsons, Jimmy and Larry Kerr, for their encouragement. And, last but not least, the author's heartfelt thanks to her husband for his expertise and advice in compiling *Texas Rose.*

Preface

Many books have been written about Texas but few tell of the children of early Texas. This book is about little Dilue Rose and her family who came to Texas in 1833 when Rose was eight years old. They settled near Harrisburg and experienced the hardships and adventures that were prevalent when Texas was struggling to win her freedom from Mexico.

Texas Rose is based upon Dilue's reminiscences of her life in the early days. She wrote her memoirs in her later years, and they were published in 1900, 1901, and 1904 issues of *The Quarterly of the Texas State Historical Association*.

The Shipwreck

"Are we going to drown?"

"Hush, Dilue! You'll scare your little sister, and you know we mustn't worry your father." Margaret Rose had difficulty controlling her voice, but she did not want her three children to know her own fears.

In spite of her mother's words, Dilue was afraid. She expected their ship to break apart any minute with the storm tossing it to and fro. The rough seas of their two-week voyage from New Orleans had been a nightmare for the passengers. Many had been violently sick. Dilue's father was the ship's only doctor. He had had very little rest. Now he suffered from seasickness and fatigue. Dilue could tell by her father's labored breathing that his fever had risen higher. He seemed too weak to lift his head.

Dilue was not the only one who was frightened. The other passengers crouched in the dark, airless quarters

1

were frightened, too. Between moans and mournful groanings from the Negro slaves, others were praying softly. The endless hours of suspense took their toll on the children. Dilue's head began to nod. It was not long before she joined her younger sister and was fast asleep.

When she awoke sometime later, Dilue knew something was different. There was silence — an eerie silence. "What is it, Gran?" she whispered, leaning closer to her brother for his protection.

"Sounds like the storm is slowing down. The sailors dropped the anchor, and Captain Denmore shouted orders for the pilot to stop anyone from jumping overboard. Guess someone was trying. Maybe the captain plans on getting us to Harrisburg after all."

"Where are we?"

Granville shrugged his shoulders. "Who knows? We are in the Gulf of Mexico somewhere."

"Aren't you afraid?"

"Not any more. The storm is almost over." The boy glanced in his mother's direction. "Uncle James has been gone a long time, hasn't he? You think I oughta go up on deck and see what's happened?"

"Well . . ." Mrs. Rose was concerned, too, that her brother had not returned. However, she was not eager for her only son to leave her sight. In her heart, Margaret Rose knew she would not be able to protect the ten-year-old much longer. Like the other settlers on board, she realized many unknown hardships and difficulties lay ahead of them. Much of Texas was still wild and unsettled in 1833.

As Granville's mother began to answer, a deafening noise drowned out her words. The sailing schooner lurched, then shook violently. It finally came to rest tilted to one side. The ship had run onto a sandbar and was stuck there. In the semidarkness the passengers

2

were panicky, unable to stand upright on their feet. Some were praying, some sobbing, others wailing.

The captain was checking the damage to the ship when he heard their cries and ordered some of his men to go to their rescue. The sailors went to work helping the passengers onto the deck. From there they were lowered over the side of the boat into the shallow water. They lost no time getting to shore. Back inside the ship, Mrs. Rose refused to leave her husband alone. Uncle James and the sailors managed to carry Dr. Rose from his sickbed to safety on land.

That night was like a bad dream. Dilue learned later that the captain had sent for help while the others had looked for shelter. They found a shack where they built a fire, then returned to save what cargo they could from the schooner. Dilue was never sure of all that happened. She only remembered sleeping on a dirt floor in her wet clothes.

Shortly after daybreak the next morning, a rescue boat came for them. When the passengers saw it, they all shook their heads. The vessel was too small to hold all of them and their belongings. The captain decided the only solution was to make two trips. The doctor and his family were with the first group. When they were finally loaded, the vessel made its way up the narrow inlet toward Harrisburg. Silently, the men studied the land along the bayou. The black earth seemed rich enough, but by the looks of the trees and mud along the banks the water had overflowed many times.

News of the shipwreck spread quickly through Harrisburg. A number of citizens lined the banks to offer assistance and a place for the victims to stay. One of the ladies, a widow named Mrs. Brewster, insisted that the doctor and his family come to her house. Once they were settled, Uncle James set out to find them a place of their own.

"Margaret," James explained to his sister sometime later, "there are few homes to rent in Harrisburg, but I found one." He paused to point to a man standing nearby. "And Mr. Lytle has offered to help us move. It is impossible to buy a wagon or cart. There just aren't any for sale!"

"How kind of you to help us, Mr. Lytle," Margaret said with a grateful smile. "Did James explain that my husband is ill? Do you think he will be comfortable in your cart?" While she talked, Margaret studied the man carefully. After all, he was the first Texan she had met face to face. He was dressed in a loose-fitting deerskin shirt, and he wore a weather-beaten hat. His unkempt hair and beard did not improve his appearance much, but she decided the man did have kindly eyes.

"Don't you worry, Ma'am, we'll fix a place for your husband. We ain't got far to go, and we'll be there in no time."

"Well . . . if you say so." Margaret tried to conceal her doubts. "We will load your cart."

The children began hauling things outside before their mother could change her mind. Mrs. Brewster insisted they make a pallet for the doctor with one of her quilts. Once that was arranged and the patient was made comfortable, the other items were tucked in around him. Margaret eyed her boxes and hoped they would not fall off, but she remained silent. Instead she looked at Mrs. Brewster and said, "How can we ever thank you?"

"You don't have to thank me, just come back and visit. You hear?" Mrs. Brewster tearfully hugged each of the children to her bosom.

"We will," Margaret replied, climbing up to sit beside Mr. Lytle in the cart. The children walked with their uncle as they started off down the unpaved street. They waved until their new friend was out of sight.

Mr. Lytle had to speak loudly to be heard above the noise of his squeaky cart. "Ya folks are mighty lucky to find a frame house. Most are made of logs."

Mrs. Rose smiled feebly. "After that boat trip I am grateful for anything. By the way, where is the church?"

"Church?" Mr. Lytle seemed surprised. "We don't have a church."

"No church? Where is the school?"

"Ain't no school neither!"

"What? No church or school?" Mrs. Rose was shocked.

Mr. Lytle peered at her curiously. "Ma'am, we ain't even got no jail! We don't need none — everybody's honest."

The woman shook her head and wondered what kind of town Harrisburg was going to be.

"Now don't ya worry," Mr. Lytle soothed, reading her thoughts. "This is a fine place. Why, we've got two dry goods stores that'll sell almost everything you'll need. We even get fresh supplies from New Orleans twice a year!"

"Only twice a year?" It was Uncle James's turn to be surprised.

"That's right. The schooners haul back hides and cotton to sell for us. Course . . . I gotta admit things sometimes do get scarce before the ships return." Noticing the worried expression on Margaret's face, Mr. Lytle quickly went on. "But just wait — ya'll will like it here."

Mrs. Rose kept her doubts to herself. Dilue, too, wondered if Mr. Lytle was right. Harrisburg certainly looked different from St. Louis, where she had spent the eight years of her young life.

5

Lost

The next few days were busy as the Roses settled into their new home. After living in St. Louis, the children were delighted with the wide openness of Texas. Granville leaped out of bed each morning to do his chores so he could go exploring with his uncle. They told the family about the strange birds and creatures they saw. The boy was glad his father was getting stronger. He wanted to share his adventures with him.

Shortly after breakfast one morning, Dilue said, "Gran says there are berries down by the fence. May we go pick some, Mother?"

"Well . . ."

"They are dewberries and they'd taste awful good." Dilue stared at the tip of her high-top shoe. "We could call it my birthday present."

"Birthday?" Her mother caught her breath trying to

recall what had happened on the twenty-eighth of April. Suddenly it all came back to her. "Mercy! You *did* have a birthday. In the excitement we forgot about it. That was the day of our shipwreck with your father so sick. No wonder we did not remember. I am just glad he is so much better now."

"That's all right."

"Goodness, Dilue, are you eight? It does not seem possible. Just look at you — you are straight as a reed! That dress was much too long when we left Missouri, but now the sleeves are too short and your ankles are showing. We can't have that!"

Dilue squirmed. She always felt nervous when people talked about her. She wanted to change the subject. "If Ella and I took the buckets we could pick lots of berries. You would like that, wouldn't you Father?" She looked to him for support.

"Please," Ella pleaded. Her father answered her with a smile.

Margaret sighed heavily as she took the wooden buckets from the shelf. She knew when she was beaten. "All right, girls, but wear your bonnets or you will be freckled like berries. And don't you go past the fence. Now I have work to do so be gone with you."

She stood at the doorway watching the girls run toward the fence. The gentle breeze blew their long hair in all directions. Margaret never ceased to marvel at the difference in the two. Some said Dilue was the spitting image of her mother, with her reddish-colored hair, clear blue-gray eyes, and fair skin. The other children had their father's dark brown eyes and hair. Their olive skin tanned a rich golden color in the sun, but poor Dilue's only blistered. Margaret shook her head, reminding herself she had work to do.

Meanwhile, the girls skipped through the soft

grasses that curled around their legs. They were delighted with the brambles loaded with plump purple berries and could not wait to try them.

"We'd better be careful, Ella, not to get our aprons or dresses messy. Mama would be mad at us."

"I'll be careful."

They went to work on the vines, putting almost as many berries into their mouths as into their buckets. After a little while, Dilue stopped to push a wisp of red hair from her eyes and looked around. That was when she saw the patch of bright blue and yellow flowers.

"Look! Let's pick some of those. Mother loves flowers. We can make a basket of our aprons like this so our hands will be free." Dilue showed her sister how to tuck the hem of her apron into the ties that went around her waist. It did not take them long to have more flowers than they could carry without them spilling over. They returned to picking berries.

After a few minutes, Ella spotted another clump of heavily laden vines farther down the way. "There are lots more over there. Come on."

They hurried in that direction and started picking. Little did they realize they were moving farther and farther away from home and were wandering deeper into the piney woods — until it was too late.

Ella was the first to look around. "I don't remember that funny tree, do you, Lue?"

Her sister stared from one tree to another. They all seemed alike but that one. "No, but we must have come that way." She pointed to the east. They took a few steps and looked around. A thick layer of leaves under their feet completely covered any signs of their footprints. The shadowy dampness of the dense woods gave Dilue a creepy feeling. Ella felt it, too.

"I'm scared."

"Come on," Dilue said, "let's go this way."

They walked side by side for a little distance and stopped again.

"I'm tired, Lue, I want to sit down."

"All right, but just for a minute." They found a dead tree which had fallen and sat on it to rest. Dilue was wondering what they should do when they heard a strange noise from nearby.

Ella began to cry, "I want to go home! I want my mama!"

"So do I but, Ella," Dilue patted her sister's hand while she talked, "I hate to say it, but I think we are lost!"

"Lost?" Ella's sobs grew louder.

"Crying won't do us any good. Come on, let's go." Dilue gathered her things and started off again. Her little sister was right behind her. Going one way and then another, the girls were weaving deeper and deeper into the woods. The thick layer of leaves overhead hid the noonday sun. On they went. They jumped in fear as the bushes directly in their path started to move. A furry animal leaped in front of them and vanished into a hole in the ground.

"Aren't we silly? That was just a little old rabbit!" Dilue hated to admit that a rabbit could scare her, but it had. What might jump out next? It could be something bigger. What could they do? She felt sure Granville would come looking for them when he discovered they were missing. That was her only hope, but with so many trees Granville might never find them. Suddenly, Dilue had an idea. "If we start yelling maybe someone will hear us."

They took turns calling, pausing afterwards to listen. No one answered. They walked slower and slower. Finally, too tired to go on, the two girls sat down to rest. With her head in her hands, Dilue fought back the tears.

It seemed the woods were closing in on them when Dilue heard a noise. About the time she thought she must have been dreaming she heard it again. Tap-tap. She decided it must be a woodpecker when she heard a dog barking and the sound of someone using an ax.

"Let's go, Ella," she cried, racing toward the sound. Before very long they came to a clearing and could see a house in the distance.

"That's not our house!" Ella whispered in despair.

"Well, there is a man — maybe he can help us. Let's see."

A big black dog barked excitedly as the girls raced toward the man. The woodcutter stopped his chopping to see what all the commotion was about. When he saw the girls he scolded the dog. "Hush, Blackie. Well, what have we here?" He looked from one tear-stained face to the other.

"Mister, will you help us? We're lost."

"Lost? Where'd you come from? I ain't seen you around here before."

"We don't know where we live."

"How come you don't?"

"Because we just moved here."

Ella began to sob again, "I want my mama."

"In a case like that, let's see what we can do." The man scratched his chin thoughtfully. "Say, you wouldn't be the new doctor's younguns, would you?"

"Yes!"

"Well, I'll be! Understand your pa rented the Robinson place, but how'd you get here? You two might get lost again findin' your way home, so I'd better walk you back. Here, give me your pails before you spill the rest of your berries. What's your name, young lady?"

"Mine's Dilue, that's Ella."

The man kept a constant stream of chatter going. He

10

reminded Dilue of Mr. Lytle, who was a big talker, too. It was when they rounded the bend in the path that she finally saw their house.

Mother was in the yard calling for them. "Dilue? Ella? Where are you?"

"Mama, Mama," the girls yelled. The man had to lengthen his steps to keep up. With a chuckle, he watched them rush into their mother's outstretched arms and, from the smile on her face, he was sure she was so relieved to have them home she would forget to be angry. They did not need to be scolded; they had learned their lesson for that day.

Wolves

In the coming months, Dilue's father recovered enough to doctor the people who came to him for help. Money was scarce, but the people paid him with what they had. The Roses were kept supplied with a variety of different foods. One person paid the doctor with five bushels of corn, which the doctor had ground into meal for bread. Mother kept it stored with the tea, rice, and white sugar they had bought in New Orleans. The children were delighted when Father brought home a pair of hunting dogs and two shiny brown horses.

Life seemed to bring one problem after the other to the settlers. The heavy rains of June caused the rivers and bayous to flood, and the waters ruined the freshly planted fields of corn. Corn was not a luxury but a necessity. It was food for the people and their animals. Before long, the corn became scarce. The high waters caused by the rains also prevented the schooner from bringing supplies from New Orleans. Soon there was a shortage of coffee and flour. They were hard to buy at any price. Then, to make matters still worse, the steam mill closed in Harrisburg, leaving the workers with no jobs.

By December, Dr. Rose decided it was time for them to move. He rented the Cartwright farm which was fifteen miles away on the Brazos River. The owner agreed to leave several cows so they could have milk and butter and cheese. Dilue's mother, who had been raised in the country, understood farm life. Her husband knew nothing about it. He could only hope things would be better there. Many of the people on the larger farms, or plantations, raised cotton and owned slaves to work the land. The Roses were not in favor of slavery; they trusted in the good Lord to help them.

When it was time for the Roses to move, Mr. Lytle came with his cart once more. Three young men who were going on to the Stafford plantation came with him. It did not take them long to get things loaded. The girls rode on the cart with their mother and Mr. Lytle. The oxen walked so slowly the men rode on ahead of the cart with the dogs. The muddy road became worse. When they came to the top of a small hill, Mr. Lytle stopped the oxen and scratched his head. "Just look at that!" he exclaimed.

The recent rains had caused the river to overflow its banks and cover most of the land in front of them. It was impossible to see the road.

"Oh, my! What will we do, Mr. Lytle?"

"Well, I reckon we'd better camp here, Missus Rose. Maybe by mornin' the water will be down and we can go on. Good thing I thought of puttin' in some kindlin'. We can at least build us a fire."

Margaret clasped her shawl as she scanned the horizon for her husband and the others. "Surely Pleasant will be back soon."

It was after dark when the men returned with plenty of wood to cook the deer they had killed. They laughed and joked as they readied the meat for roasting. With their talking and the cheery fire, Dilue forgot about their dismal surroundings until, suddenly, she felt she was being watched. Dilue turned slowly to peer into the shadows behind her. What she saw sent chills up her spine. There were eyes — hundreds of eyes — everywhere she looked! Once she found her voice she began to scream.

The men grabbed their guns and spun around. Mr. Lytle shouted a warning before anyone could speak. "Look out — those are wolves! A pack of hungry wolves!" He dashed for his oxen while Uncle James ran to bring the horses nearer to the fire. Meanwhile, Granville and his father fastened the hunting dogs under the cart and Margaret crawled up into the cart. The girls decided the safest place for them was with their mother.

"Don't shoot!" Mr. Lytle warned, as he threw more wood onto the fire. "No tellin' what them critters will do if they get a taste of blood." The wolves apparently understood his words. They howled in protest.

An uneasy silence fell upon the group. Father attempted to sound confident when he said, "Now, children, we will be all right, don't you worry."

"How can you say that, Pleasant?" mother groaned. "We are surrounded by wolves and there is water everywhere. Just look — that tree is loaded with birds waiting to pick our bones when daylight comes!"

Dilue eyed the nearby tree and shivered. Her mother was right. The tree was alive with buzzards. They were sleeping, but what would they do in the morning?

There was little thought of sleep. The men stood

guard while the girls huddled beside their mother in the cart. That night was one of horrors for them all.

The group watched the last of the wood burn to ashes and waited nervously for the light of day. When it came, Dilue realized her prayers had been answered. The wolves had disappeared, the buzzards had vanished, and the water had gone down. She rubbed her eyes in disbelief. The night might never have happened except for the animal tracks in the mud. However, the men were taking no chances. They broke camp before anything else could occur.

Sometime later they reached the place Father had rented from the Cartwright family. The two-story log house was not exactly what Margaret had expected, but she was too tired to argue. She went in without a word. Once they were inside, Father bragged on the big fireplace along one wall and the two heavy wooden doors at either end of the downstairs room. Mother could not help but notice the ladder needed to get to the rooms in the attic. She could only hope someone would not break a leg climbing up to bed, but she kept that thought to herself.

Slaves

Life on the farm was very different from life in Harrisburg. There were no other houses in sight, and there was work to do from morning to night. After the cows were milked and the animals fed, Granville and his father went to the fields with Uncle James to start the plowing and planting. The girls washed the dishes and helped with the cleaning while Mother made their beds and put on something to cook for lunch. Dilue and her sister spent the afternoons learning to card cotton to be used for ploughlines or woven into cloth. It was a new life for everyone.

One Sunday in mid-February, Father said, "You girls go wash your faces and get your bonnets. Granville is saddling the horses to take you to see the neighbor children."

Dilue and Ella squealed in delight and ran to get

16

their hats. The only children anywhere around were the Roarks, who lived two miles away. They had been to visit the Roses once. After the Roarks were gone, Dilue's parents spoke of how the father, Elijah Roark, had been scalped by the Indians. That had happened a few months before the youngest child was born. Little Mary was five years old and had never seen her father. Dilue shivered at the thought and felt sorry for Mary. The older boys, Leo and Jackson, worked the Roark farm while the nine-year-old twins, Louise and Lucenda, helped their mother around the house. The idea of going for a visit was most exciting to Dilue.

Once they were ready, Father seated the girls in front of Granville on the horse. He then handed him the reins and said, "Be careful, but hurry back with Mrs. Roark, son."

With those instructions, they were off. Dilue felt so at ease on a horse she could not wait for the time when Father would let her ride by herself.

Dilue was beginning to wonder if they were lost when she saw the Roarks' house. The children had seen them coming and were waiting out in the yard with their mother.

"Well, looky who's here," Mrs. Roark exclaimed as she helped the girls to the ground. "Come on in, boy, and sit a spell."

"No, Ma'am, I can't," Granville replied, shaking his head. "Father sent me to get you and he said for us to hurry."

"I reckoned it was about that time. Guess we had better be going. Girls, you behave yourselves until I get back."

Mrs. Roark could have saved her breath. The children were delighted to have visitors. The twins entertained Dilue and her sister by showing them the house and the vegetable garden, but it was too muddy to go down to Oyster Creek to see the fish. It seemed they had just started playing when their mother returned. The day had gone much too quickly for them all. With hugs and farewell kisses, the girls promised to return soon.

Father was waiting for them when they got home. "Come on in, children, but don't slam the door. Your mother and I have something to show you. But do not make any noise. Come on, she is in bed."

They crowded around to look at the bundle in the crook of Margaret's arm. "What do you think of your baby sister, girls?" her voice sounded tired. "We are trying to decide on a name. What do you think we should call her, Dilue?"

"I don't know," Dilue whispered. She had forgotten how small a newborn baby could be. As she watched, the baby wrinkled its button nose and opened its rosebud mouth in a yawn. "If we named her Louisiana we could call her Ana — that is a nice name. What do you think, Father?"

"I would like to call her Texas, but your mother doesn't like that. What do you think, Gran?"

"Well . . ." the boy sounded thoughtful, "how about Missouri?"

Ella giggled, "If we name her that I'll call her Missy!"

Mother smiled at the name. "Missy? I like that. Pleasant, let's call her Missouri." No one ever called Father by his real name but Mother.

"All right, Missouri it is. Now, I am hungry. Let's find something to eat before we go to bed. It has been a long day."

A few days later the weather turned cold. In spite of the chilling wind, father insisted the fields had to be readied for planting. The men had not been gone from the house long when Dilue glanced out the window and caught her breath. "Mother, what's that?"

Margaret took one look, dropped the broom, and screamed, "Indians! Granville, get your father — *quick!*" She clutched the baby to her bosom and fought the urge to run into the woods with the girls.

Before Granville could leave, his father and Uncle James burst into the room. "Margaret, those aren't Indians — they are Negro slaves! James and I will go see what they want. Son, stay here with your mother until we get back." The doctor was gone before his wife could open her mouth to protest.

Many hours later the two men returned with their clothes spattered with blood. The family was relieved to hear it was only blood from a cow. "James, we might as well sit down and tell them what has happened." They all found a place to sit and listen to Father's story. "Well, it seems Ben Smith — he's the owner of those Negroes — and two other white men left Galveston to go to Smith's plantation. Somehow they got lost and have been wandering around ever since. Those poor black people are half dead and are wearing so few clothes they are freezing."

"That is right, Margaret," James said, ignoring the expression on his sister's face. "We killed two cows to cook for them, but they ate them raw — like hungry dogs!"

"Oh, the poor things," whispered Dilue.

Uncle James went on. "Smith has asked me to stand watch tonight so he and his men can get some sleep. From the looks of those Negroes they will not need much watching. They are completely tuckered out."

"But where did they come from?"

"Africa, I guess. They do not seem to speak or understand English. Of course, we know smuggling and trading slaves is illegal in Texas, but it seems to be happening anyway." James took his gun and headed for the door. "Margaret, keep the girls away from the windows until Smith gets some clothes for those men from his place. You hear?" From their faces he knew he did not need to say more. The womenfolk had no intention of looking out the window.

Dilue had trouble going to sleep that night. She kept thinking about the Negroes. There was something about slavery that bothered her.

Several days later, a wagon came from the Smiths' place with clothing for the slaves. Before they could dress, they were marched to the creek for a bath. Once they were clean and dressed, Mr. Smith brought them up to the house for the doctor's family to see. No one said a word. Dilue studied one face after another. The sad expression in their eyes haunted her for days. Even at her age, Dilue was sure slavery was wrong.

Settling Down

In the days and weeks that followed, Dr. Rose had many visitors. Dilue didn't understand all their talk, but she knew there was trouble brewing when the men talked of the Mexican government not abiding by the Constitution of 1824. They talked of Stephen F. Austin being kept in a jail in Mexico City by the Mexican President Santa Anna.

The Roses had no way of knowing that some of their visitors would play an important role in the future of Texas. Dilue only knew she liked the white-haired man with the long beard, the one Father called David Burnet. Granville made friends with a fellow who had a wooden leg. Most people called him "Three-legged Willie," but Dilue preferred to call him Mr. Williamson until the day he brought her a gift of side combs for her long hair. After that, he was Mr. Willie to her.

Dilue's favorite visitor was Col. William Barret Travis. He was a young lawyer who, like Dilue, had bright red hair. He was not a frequent visitor, but she looked forward to his coming — especially after he sent the girls Sunday school books back from San Felipe. Mr. Travis promised to buy them a Bible, but he sent back word there were none for sale. Mother was disappointed about that, for she wanted one.

Early one morning in April, a neighbor sent word that everyone was invited to a dance that evening. The thought of a party was most exciting. It meant the girls could take a bath and wash their hair.

From the way the people looked at them on the way to the party, Dilue was sure they were quite a sight riding in their sleigh. Father laughed that others rode in wagons and carts, but the Roses were the only ones in the neighborhood with a snow sleigh.

It was almost dark when they arrived at the party. The Dyer family's cabin had a festive glow once the candles were lighted. By the time the fiddler started to play the song "Pine Woods," people were ready to dance.

Dilue was surprised that the Stafford boy came over and said, "Would you like to dance the Virginia reel with me?"

Before she could explain she did not know how to dance, Dilue found herself whirling around the floor. Soon her sister was dancing with another young man. There were many more boys than girls, so even the smallest young ladies were asked to dance. The stomping and shuffling went on and on and on. Dilue danced to every song. Hours later, the party finally came to an end. Day was breaking when everyone headed home, tired, but happy. It had been a night Dilue would always remember.

Margaret Rose worried about a number of things: floods, snakes, Indians, and storms. But the thing that concerned her most was the lack of a school. She often said, "Our children can read. That is why I have them keep up with their studies. All children should learn to read."

On one of Father's frequent trips to Harrisburg, he saw a redheaded fellow step off a boat which had just arrived from New Orleans. When he learned that the Irishman, David Henson, was a teacher looking for a school, Dilue's father offered him a job. Of course, there was a problem: there was no school building. They did have a one-room cabin that had been used as a blacksmith's shop. It had no windows or doors, but Father decided it would do until a better one could be built. Mother was delighted with the idea and encouraged Granville to spread the news.

The school opened the first day of June with seven pupils — five boys of varying sizes and Dilue and her sister. When the teacher asked who could read and write, only two raised their hands: Dilue and Granville.

Mr. Henson was a good teacher. Dilue could not help feeling sorry for him though. Without books, his job was not easy. However, he taught the students to read and write their names before school let out in August. The time in school was short because the boys were needed in the fields to pick the cotton. The girls looked forward to returning the next June.

Indians

One morning in late November, Father reached for his gun and hat. "I guess I am ready to leave for Brazoria to sell our cotton. Granville, your Uncle James is going along to help the widow lady, so you will be the man of the house while we are gone."

"How long will that be?"

"I am not sure, son. A lot depends on the roads. You should not have any trouble — you are pretty smart, for a twelve-year-old."

Dilue knew her mother wasn't happy before she asked, "Do you have to go, Pleasant?"

"Now, honey, you know we need the money. Besides, all the other men are going, and there is no one to go in my place. Granville is not strong enough to handle that load of cotton. Now don't you worry, we will be back as soon as possible." Father headed out the door hand in

24

hand with Mother. The children trailed along behind. With a kiss for each and a wave of his hand, Father headed the oxen down the road. The cotton piled high on the sleigh made it look like an enormous snowball rolling behind the oxen. The family stood and watched Father until he faded from sight.

A few days later, Granville crawled from his warm, cozy bed to face the chilly December morning. He was still half asleep when he climbed down the ladder from their bedroom in the attic and tossed some logs into the fireplace. He fanned the embers with his hand until they began to burn. Mother was making the coffee when he took the bucket and started out the door to milk the cows. He stopped with a jolt. What he saw made his eyes open wide. The wooden bucket dropped from his hand with a crash.

In the wooded area down the road were Indians — hundreds of them! Granville made a beeline back into the house and slammed the door yelling, *"Jumpin' Jehoshaphat!* Bolt the windows — quick! There's Indians out there!"* He caught a glimpse of his sister starting down the ladder and shouted, "Lue, stay up there with Ella and the baby. Mother, maybe you had better go back up there, too."

Margaret reached for the old gun Father kept on the wall and shook her head. "Don't you worry about me. Since we got to Texas I have faced a flood, hungry buzzards, and a pack of wolves. We will face these Indians together, son."

They poked their gun barrels through the cracks in the walls and waited. Over on one side of the Indians they could see a herd of ponies. The woods were swarming with men, women, and children who apparently had no thought of scalping the Rose family. In fact, the Indians seemed to be setting up camp to stay for a while.

"Did you ever see so many Indians? Must be 300 or more. What'll we do? There are not any men left around here — they have all taken their cotton to market. I can't go for help. I am about the oldest fellow around here since Leo Roark went with them to Brazoria."

"We will just wait, Gran, and see what happens."

And wait they did. One hour, then two. It was bad enough listening to the cows bawling to be milked and the pig squealing for her food, but when the baby started crying for her breakfast, Granville got nervous. Before he could make a move to do something, he realized one of the Indian women was heading in their direction. Granville looked down the sight of his musket but, before he could pull the trigger, his mother spoke up. "Don't shoot. She has no gun. Let's wait and see what she wants."

The Indian stopped and raised her hands before she reached the house. She seemed to be looking right at Granville when she said, "No shoot. We Wacos — good Indians — friends."

"Why, she's talking English," Granville exclaimed under his breath. He had heard of people being robbed and scalped because they believed an Indian who said he was a friend. He did not bat an eye or move his finger from the gun trigger.

"Corn. Want corn — hungry."

Margaret weighed the situation in her mind and finally decided the best thing might be to give her corn. After all, Margaret reasoned, the woman seemed harmless enough, and no one in the camp was making a move to come their way. Margaret put down her gun and took some corn from the storage bin. Granville did not move a muscle until his mother returned from giving the corn to the woman. Sometime later, the Indian returned with a pair of brightly decorated moccasins and left them on the porch. The girls were disappointed. The shoes were too

26

large for them, but they fit their mother's feet like gloves.

After that, Margaret said she was not afraid. She declared that if Indians were minding their business, the children should do the same. Dilue found that wasn't easy. She kept remembering Elijah Roark's scalping and the stories of whole settlements being burned out by wild Indians. But by the time Father got home, they had grown accustomed to the Indian camp in the woods. They felt proud when he bragged on them for being so brave.

The rains of January and February came and went. The first warm days of March caused the prairies to explode into an array of brightly colored flowers. There was no doubt but that spring was in the air.

Mother and the girls were in the yard washing the clothes as they usually did on Monday. Dilue was the first to notice something strange happening in the Indian camp. The Indian women were busy as beavers, loading blankets, skins, pots, and kettles onto their ponies. They fastened baskets filled with children to some of the horses. The mothers with little babies wore them tied to a board on their backs.

On a signal from their chief, the men began to move through the woods. The women and loaded horses were not far behind. The Indian dogs brought up the rear. Like a column of soldiers going to war, the Indians marched away leaving a feeling of great relief and peace in the hearts of the Roses and Roarks. Dilue was happy the Indians had gone.

Time to Celebrate

"Now you girls stay near your mother for the next three days. If we got separated I would never know how to find you here in Harrisburg — not in this crowd."

Mother looked at the sea of faces milling around the camp and shook her head. "I am not sure, Pleasant, that any Fourth of July celebration is worth all this excitement."

Father patted her hand. "Margaret, we have planned on this barbeque for weeks. Why, the girls even have new dresses!"

"And the ball — don't forget the ball!"

"How could I forget, Dilue? You have talked of nothing else, but it looks as if you will have to wait another day to dance. Today's the day for speeches. And, with all the talk of President Santa Anna's soldiers causing trouble over duty from the goods coming in by schooner, the speeches should be good. We will go listen to those, Granville, and give your mother a chance to visit with some of the women. She is not interested in politics." He could have added that Dilue was not interested either, but he did not.

When they returned sometime later, Father told them a man had died and was to be buried in the morning. There would be no music or dancing, out of respect to the dead, until the next evening after they had eaten. Dilue was sorry about the man, but she was disappointed there would not be more time for dancing.

The next morning everyone, including a number of Mexican soldiers who had come to the celebration, attended the funeral. Mr. Choate read a long burial message and someone sang a song. After it was over, Father whispered that the Mexican officer shaking hands with a group of men standing nearby was Captain Tenorio.

The sun was going down when the crowd headed for the dance area. A new storehouse was being used for the occasion. The musicians were instructed to play only waltzes since the Mexican officers did not know the country dances. Few people danced when the music first started. But Captain Tenorio and a beautiful German lady made the waltz look so simple, everyone was eager to try. Dilue loved dancing! She had no trouble learning the steps. Before the night was over, she was one of the most popular girls at the ball. The light of day was peeking over the trees when the musicians played the final song.

With the celebration over, the young people headed home weary but happy. Their parents, however, went home feeling nervous over all the talk of war and trouble with Mexico.

In the coming months there was more talk of fighting. It was rumored that Santa Anna was preparing to liberate the Negro slaves and drive out anyone who spoke against the Mexican government. This was dangerous talk. The plantation owners felt very strongly that they had a right to own slaves. They had paid good money for the slaves who worked their fields. Without the Negroes, who would pick their cotton or till their land? Some of the older settlers were opposed to any talk of war, but the younger ones were eager for a fight.

When September rolled around, one of the Roses' frequent visitors reported that Stephen Austin had just returned to San Felipe after his release from jail. Austin did not look well; his friends were concerned about his health. Many felt Austin was the one man who knew what was best for Texas. Dilue could not imagine spending two years in a dingy prison cell. Just the thought of it made her feel sorry for Austin.

# The Bear

The Roses looked forward to their occasional visitors. They usually brought interesting news or had stories to share. It was not often any of them needed the doctor's medical advice, but one man did.

Late one afternoon, Granville and his father were plowing in the field when they saw a lone rider coming their way. The man was having trouble staying on his horse.

"Wonder what's wrong?"

"Guess we had better go see, son. Besides, it is almost quitting time."

Their visitor slid from his horse and fell to the ground as they left the field. Father hurried ahead, leaving Granville to handle the oxen and plow. By the time Granville got there, the man was sitting up. He seemed dazed. His old deerskin shirt was ripped in several places.

"Give me a hand, son, and let's get him into the house."

They managed to get the man to his feet, but he was unable to walk without their help. Before they reached the porch, Father shouted, "Margaret, open the door for us."

"What's wrong?" She had already opened the door.

"I can't be sure until I have checked him over. Let's put him on the floor in front of the hearth, son. He might fall out of a chair — he looks pretty muddled. Dilue, will you light the candles while your brother helps me get off his shirt? And, Ella, you get something to put under his head for a pillow."

While he talked, the doctor's experienced hands were feeling for broken bones or wounds. Once he had completed his examination, he sighed. "Well, apparently he hasn't any broken bones, just these scratches on his arms. One of you bring some water and something for me to clean them with."

While Dilue filled the basin with water, her mother looked for cloths. Father looked at the man's shirt more closely. "Unless I miss my guess, these rips were made by a claw of some kind — probably from a bear."

Granville leaned over for a closer look. "Really?"

"Do not get in the light, Gran, move back. Margaret, would you please fetch my spirits? You know where I keep them. I'll use some on these cuts and, from the looks of him, I think this fellow could use a little sip."

Mother handed him the alcohol without a word. After Father forced the man to swallow a few drops, it was not long before his glassy stare began to fade and the color returned to his face. He sputtered and coughed a few times. The doctor made him swallow more. "That's enough," he protested feebly. "I ain't a heavy drinker."

Father handed the spirits back to mother, chuckling softly, "I'm not either, but there is a time when it comes in mighty handy — like now. I will just clean you up a little, Mister, then we will let you rest." All the time he talked, Father was working on the man. When he finished, he rocked back on his heels, studying his patient. Although he was conscious, he stared blankly at the ceiling. "Son, give me a hand and we will put on his shirt so he won't catch a cold. That floor is cold. Dilue, how about getting our patient some coffee? He looks like he could use it." Dilue jumped up to pour the coffee.

"Ella, you girls wash your hands and help me get supper on the table. There is nothing more we can do for our guest for now," Mother said.

"You are right — he may be hungry after a little while. Granville, since the womenfolk are busy fixing supper we might as well go see about the oxen."

When they returned a short time later, the patient seemed better. He was leaning against the hearth watching the girls set the table. He insisted on sitting in a chair when everything was ready. After they had eaten and the visitor's coffee cup had been refilled, the children waited expectantly to hear his story. Father tossed several logs on the fire, moved the candles to the center of the long table, and sat down. Once he was seated comfortably in his place, he cleared his throat and said, "My name's Rose — Doctor Rose — and this is my family. Good thing you came when you did, Mister. You were tuckered out."

"Reckon you would like to know what happened, wouldn't you?"

They nodded.

He shook his head like he was shaking the cobwebs

away. "Reckon I'm purty lightheaded, but I'll try. My name's Morrill, and I'm a Baptist preacher."

Mother's eyes sparkled at having a minister in their house and hung onto his every word. The man did not sound like any preacher Dilue ever heard in Missouri. She decided Texas pastors had a different way of talking.

"I was down at the riverbottom huntin' for deer and turkey. The weeds down there are mighty high — some's over my head in places."

They shook their heads. They had hunted in the riverbottom, too.

"I'm always on the lookout for Injuns, so I was goin' along real slow like. All of a sudden, ol' Bess — that's my horse — laid back her ears and got a wild look in her eyes. I was fussin' with her when, about forty steps in front of us, there appeared this great big ol' bear standin' on its hind legs comin' right at us. Bess was actin' so skittish I couldn't even shoot."

Dilue thought her brother would have a fit for sure when the preacher paused to sip his coffee. But he did not. "I jumped to the ground and was takin' aim when Bess jarred my arm, so that I dropped the reins. I made a grab for 'em but lost my balance and fell. It was too late to catch that horse. She'd run off behind a clump of trees. About that time, I heard a growl. The weeds snapped and shook. I figured I'd better get ready — it was comin' right at me."

Mr. Morrill paused again to catch his breath. No one moved. They waited breathlessly for the story to go on.

"Sure enough — she come right outa the weeds with her ears laid back and her mouth wide open, lookin' like somethin' out of the pits of hell! Let me tell you, my legs was jelly. I was shakin' so bad I couldn't keep the barrel steady to aim and fire." His eyes rolled heavenward as he continued. "But the good Lord was with me. That critter

34

wasn't more than eight steps away when I pulled the trigger. That ol' bear just keep on comin' with its arms spread out! I heard my shirt rippin' just before it knocked me down. No tellin' how long I laid there, but when I come to, that critter was on the ground beside me!"

"And then — " Granville could not wait for the man to finish his coffee.

"Then was when I moved — real fast! While I fumbled tryin' to reload my gun, I was keepin' an eye on that varmint. It didn't move. It was dead! Once I saw that, I yelled for ol' Bess. When she finally came, I managed to get on her somehow. Next thing I knew, I was here!" The preacher heaved a heavy sigh muttering under his breath, "Thank the Lord."

"*Jumpin' Jehoshaphat!* What a story!" Granville could not help slapping his leg for emphasis. "Say, where is that bear?"

Mr. Morrill rubbed his chin thoughtfully. "That is a good question."

"If I find that bear, can I keep the hide?"

"Sonny," the preacher said, "I ain't got no money to pay your pa for his work, but I reckon that skin is worth a purty penny at the market. How about we say it's payment for all your help?"

"You do not have to pay us," Father replied. But, seeing Granville's disappointment, he added, "however, if you insist. I guess we could try to find that bear and skin it. You could have the meat, and we would keep the hide."

"That's a deal."

"Come on, son, we will take the hounds to help us find the bear."

It was after dark when the two returned. From Granville's expression, there was little doubt that they had found it. Father carried the light outside so they could see the skin stretched out on the ground to dry. Dilue felt sure it was big enough to make Mother a coat.

"Mr. Morrill, you are in no shape to travel. You must spend the night with us. Besides, Pleasant will want to examine you again in the morning. Preacher," Mother lowered her eyes to stare at the floor. "One of the things I have missed in Texas is having a pastor pray with us. Would you pray with us before we go to bed?"

"I'd be proud to, Mrs. Rose." They bowed their heads while he prayed. He closed by saying, "Bless this family and put thy guardian angels around this home."

Dilue often recalled those words in the days that followed.

The next morning the Roses were sorry to say good-bye to the preacher. They made him promise to come back someday for a visit.

Buffaloes

Dilue glanced up from the boiling pot to the cloudless sky overhead and pushed a strand of hair from her moist forehead. She wondered if it would ever be cool weather again. Beads of perspiration trickled down Dilue's neck and back while she leaned over the fire to stir the bubbling mixture in the pot.

How many times in the last two years she had heard Mother say, "Good soap is like good cheese; it must be prepared just right. Too much lye added to the tallow and fat and it will separate. The coals must be real hot so the soap will simmer good. Even the stirring is important when you are making soap — not too fast and not too slow — just kind of easy like until it comes to a rolling boil. That is when you start adding the water a little at a time. You will know it is done when it's thick like jelly. It will fall apart later when you are washing if it's too runny.

That mixture is hot! When you are pouring it into that flat pan, always remember to be careful."

Dilue's thoughts wandered back to the day they moved into this two-story house on the Brazos River and all the things she had learned since then. She could not help feeling a little smug. She had learned to use honey to make jelly from many strange things like mesquite beans and cactus pears and even agarita berries. Her father's favorite was the grape jelly. It did taste mighty good when there was enough corn for bread, which had not been too often in the last few months.

Mother had taught the girls how to make bread by mixing bacon drippings with ground corn and water. It was "ash bread" when they baked it in the hot ashes on the fireplace hearth, and "corn pone" when it cooked in a pan.

One day, as they were twisting cotton into thread to weave into cloth, Margaret said, "My mama, God rest her soul, always told me a girl ought to be able to do everything around the house by the time she is twelve years old. One of these days you girls will be getting married and having children of your own. So now is the time to listen good."

Dilue giggled at the idea of getting married, and she thought of William, the oldest Dyer boy. He was eleven, a year older than Dilue. She knew with the shortage of women in Texas, some girls were brides by the time they were thirteen. Although she liked William, Dilue felt sure they were much too young to think of marriage.

The first days of October brought cooler weather and more rumors of trouble with Santa Anna. Father said he had heard so many different reports he did not know what to believe any more. They learned the one about the

Mexican army heading for Texas was true. News came that General Cos and his troops were in San Antonio.

"There is going to be trouble for sure," Dr. Rose kept saying.

How right he was! Another messenger rode by and stopped long enough to rest his horse. He said, "Did you hear about the battle at Gonzales?"

"What happened?" Father asked.

"The Mexican soldiers tried to take a cannon used for protection against the Indians, but the men of Gonzales refused to give the cannon up. They sent to the other settlements for help and, by the time help got to Gonzales, they had put a "Come and Take It" flag on the cannon. The bunch of them stood their ground." The rider ran his fingers through his unruly hair and continued. "When the Mexicans saw the Texans' guns, they started running. Reckon they didn't want that little old cannon bad enough to fight for it. But the folks of Gonzales did. Fact is, they followed the soldiers all the way to San Antonio and, from the last I heard, are planning an attack. Well, that's about all I know. Reckon I had better be on my way."

Dr. Rose went around after that looking gloomy like the weather. As if the report from San Antonio was not enough, they heard the schooner could not travel up the Brazos because the water in the river was too low.

That was when Dilue's father decided to postpone his trip to Brazoria to do some trading. He wanted to help Granville practice his shooting. With him away so often seeing to his patients and making trips to town, Father said it was important that his son knew how to handle a gun to protect the family.

"Oh, Pleasant," Mother said when she heard about it. "What kind of place is this where little boys have to carry a gun? Maybe we had better just pack up and move back to Missouri." Dilue noticed how quickly her father changed the subject. Mother was easily upset now that she was going to have another baby.

Dilue thought it strange that her mother talked about Dilue getting married, and yet Granville — who was two years older — was called a little boy.

During the night of December 4, Dilue heard her parents talking, but she was too sleepy to listen. The next morning, Father was waiting when they climbed down from their attic room. "Children, we have an early Christmas present — another baby girl. We have named her Elba."

Granville rolled his eyes in disgust. "Not another girl!"

Father could not keep from laughing. "Just look at Mr. Choate — he has *seven* daughters!"

"And now we have four girls and only that old sleigh to haul them in!"

"That is true. With four daughters I will have to think of getting a wagon. But right now, our sleigh is loaded with skins to be traded for medicine and lead and powder. I will have to go all the way to Brazoria, since boats can't make it up the river to Harrisburg. Some of those pelts, like panther and bear, should be pretty valuable. While I am gone, son, you take care of the family." Before he left, he added, "I will be back as soon as possible."

During the days he was gone, life went on just the same. When Father did return, he was bubbling with news. "General Cos surrendered in San Antonio and has been sent back across the Rio Grande River to Mexico with his men. I trust that is the last we'll hear of Cos."

Things settled back to normal along the Brazos River. Folks went about their chores with a peaceful feeling in their hearts.

One morning before dawn, Dilue heard a rumbling

40

noise that made her jump out of bed. Father heard it, too. "Go back to sleep, Lue," he whispered. But she noticed he took his gun and went outside. Later, when she did get out of bed, Dilue glanced out of the window. She could not believe her eyes. There were hundreds and hundreds of huge wooly animals everywhere she looked.

"Mama, do you see what I see?"

"Yes, buffaloes!" her mother answered nervously. "Pleasant and your brother have been on the porch watching them for hours. Let us hope those animals do not come any closer to the house. Your father said for us to stay inside. He doesn't know what they will do."

There was something majestic, yet frightening, about those shaggy buffaloes. Perhaps it was their horns and powerful shoulders — or their size. Dilue liked animals that were soft and fuzzy. The buffalo wandering slowly by their house seemed harmless enough, but there was something else worrying Dilue. She had always heard that where there were buffaloes there would usually be Indians nearby. She watched the huge animals plodding in the direction of the coast. But there was not an Indian in sight.

"Get away from that window, Dilue," Mother sighed. "We have work to do."

In the hours that followed, the girls tried not to look out the window but, with the never ending thud of hooves going past, that was not easy. Father later told them the animals seemed undisturbed by his efforts to shoo them away. They continued on to the southeast at their own pace. All that day and into the night they marched by. In the wee hours of morning, the sound finally faded away.

When daylight came, the Roses went out to survey the damage the buffalo had done to their fields. Father said there must have been 3,000 animals in all, from the way the ground was plowed.

41

For many nights after that, Dilue dreamed about buffaloes and Indians. She would awaken in a cold sweat and wonder if her mother was right. Perhaps they should move back to Missouri.

War

"Do you ever feel afraid, Mother?"

"Why do you ask, Dilue?"

Margaret studied her daughter closely. The faded dress Dilue now wore did little to hide her maturing figure. Margaret sighed deeply. Her daughter was no longer a child. "You have growing pains, young lady, that is all."

Dilue concentrated on the cotton she was carding. She found it difficult to explain her feelings but, somehow, things were different. Of course, there was more work with the new baby and, with the two orphan boys Father had hired to help in the fields, more cooking. The boys were named Alexander and William. Alexander was fifteen; his brother William was eleven. The boys were a big help, but they thought only of food and war.

War! That was what frightened Dilue the most; yet,

there was talk of little else. Messengers going from San Felipe to Brazoria and Harrisburg paused at the Rose place to rest and water their horses. They reported the possibility of Mexican ships blocking the schooners carrying cargo to and from New Orleans. Those reports had everyone nervous.

Dilue's mind wandered back to the courier who had stopped a few days earlier. He was en route to Brazoria with the latest news of the Alamo. He carried a letter from Colonel Travis asking for reinforcements because he and over 150 men were under siege by General Santa Anna's army. The Mexicans outnumbered Travis's Texans ten to one. That message did little to calm Dilue's fears.

"Sounds like someone just rode into the yard," Mother said. Dilue realized she had been daydreaming as she put aside her carding to follow her mother outside. There sat Mrs. Stafford and her child on one horse. Her son Harvey rode another. A short distance away a young black mother and her two small children sat in an ox cart.

"Margaret," the woman's voice was flat. "We have come to say goodbye."

"Goodbye? Where are you going?"

"East — to the States. Where it is safe. And we are not the only ones. With the news about Travis and his handful of men at the Alamo, some of the settlers around Goliad and San Patricio are worried. They have grabbed what they could and are fleeing. Almost everybody is talking of running from Santa Anna. You had better not stay here. This place could be a battlefield before long!" With a nod of her head, Mrs. Stafford wheeled her horse around and shouted back over her shoulder, "Better start packing soon."

"But . . . the Indians . . ." Margaret's words faded to a

whisper as her friend rode away. They watched them ride on down the road to join a group that had been waiting. "She must be wrong," Margaret mumbled to herself.

Later, a rider brought news about the delegates meeting at Washington-on-the-Brazos to talk of freedom from Mexico. They had signed a Declaration of Independence on March 2 and elected David Burnet to serve as president. Gen. Sam Houston was to act as commander in chief of the Texas army that was being formed. That news spread like wildfire. A number of men, including Uncle James and neighbors Dyer, Bell, and Neal, left their families to join Houston. The general was reportedly on his way to Gonzales to meet his troops.

Seldom a day passed that they didn't hear some story about the Mexican army. The Roses did not know what to believe. There were rumors of Santa Anna planning to march his army through Texas. In spite of the many frightening tales they heard, life went on just the same. Dr. Rose and others continued planting their corn while their women packed the family possessions to be ready to flee at a moment's notice.

With a report that Col. James Fannin's 500 men were marching from Goliad to the Alamo in San Antonio, and that Sam Houston's army now numbered over a thousand men, Father felt certain the Mexican army would never reach the Colorado River without being stopped. After all, San Antonio was more than 150 miles away. It seemed Father was right — at first.

On the morning of March 15, Granville was working in the field when he saw a rider galloping at full speed toward their place. Father saw him, too. They dropped everything and raced for the house. The rider had paused at their watering trough long enough for his horse to get a drink and to catch its breath.

When they were near enough to be heard, Granville shouted, "What's wrong?"

"Did you hear? The Alamo fell!"

"The Alamo fell?"

"Yes. Travis and all his men are dead!"

"Dead?" Granville's eyes were like saucers.

"*All* of 'em! And General Houston's retreating this way. He has given orders for everybody to run for their lives. Our folks are callin' it the Runaway Scrape. Well, I can't take time to jaw no longer." He spun his horse around and was on his way once more.

Father and son flew into the house before the courier was out of sight. The family was dazed when Father began rattling off orders like a general preparing for battle. "Granville, hitch the oxen to the sleigh! Dilue, you and Ella help your mother load the bedding and provisions. Missy, stay out of their way and watch the baby. Alexander, I am counting on you getting word to Mr. Bundick so he'll be waiting at the Roark place with the cart. He said we could use it if there was trouble. Once we get there we will shift things from our sleigh into his cart. Now, be on your way, boy." Alexander raced out the door before Father could catch his breath.

"Now, Margaret, after the sleigh is loaded, start moving. Meanwhile, I will saddle the horses and round up what cows I can. We will meet again down the road between here and the Roark house." Father squashed his floppy hat on his head on the way to the door.

Mother and the girls worked like bees swarming around a hive, piling their clothing and supplies onto the sleigh. Finally, when the load seemed ready to topple, Margaret declared, "That is all we had better try to put on. We may have too much now for one yoke of oxen. Ella, you and Missy crawl up there in the middle to keep things from sliding off. Do you girls have your bonnets?"

46

Dilue shook her head and smiled at her mother thinking of their hats when the world was coming apart.

"We will take turns carrying the baby, Dilue, while Granville drives the oxen. I guess that's everything. Let's go. It will be dark before we know it." With one fleeting glance in the direction of the house, Margaret clasped the baby to her bosom and walked away.

The little group trudged along in silence. Their spirits were as black as the moonless night creeping in around them. Dilue fought back tears when she heard her mother's gentle voice humming an old, old song. Margaret always said the blackest of things seemed to brighten with a tune. This was a time when they needed all the help they could get. Dilue had always figured there could never be a night of horrors like the ones with the shipwreck and the wolves. She was wrong. This was worse. They were running for their very lives. Dilue had never known such fear.

They had gone only a little way when Father caught up with them. He insisted on Mother riding, and he would walk with Dilue. Once Margaret was seated in the saddle, he handed the reins of the other horse to Granville.

"Son, I hate to split up the family on a night like this, but Adam Stafford needs help. You know, with his crippled leg he will never be able to get his cattle across the San Jacinto River alone. If you cut across the field heading east, you can catch up with him. We should meet up with you on the other side of the river sometime tomorrow."

Dilue swallowed the lump that formed in her throat as she watched her brother melt into the shadows. She could not stop her tears.

It was much later when they reached the Roark place to find several other families already there, including Mr. Bundick with his cart. It did not take them long to move the family's possessions from the sleigh to the cart.

"Friends," Dr. Rose said slowly, realizing there were only women and children in the group. He and Mr. Bundick were the only men; the others had joined Sam Houston's army. "We will spend the night here and move out early in the morning. We all need some sleep. It has been a hard day and there's no telling what is ahead of us."

At daybreak the next morning, the party was ready to travel. In spite of his poor health, Mr. Bundick insisted on riding his horse. Mrs. Bundick and a Negro servant rode horseback. A gray-haired Negro with a kindly voice drove the cart while Margaret and the girls sat in the back. "You all follow me," Father ordered as he took the lead.

They had gone a short distance when Dilue glanced back at the sleigh they were leaving behind. She felt silly, but she wanted to cry again. It seemed she was always crying. Seeing their sleigh standing all alone was like forsaking an old friend. She had to cry about that.

It was not long before Mr. Cotie overtook them in his large blue wagon pulled by six yoke of oxen. He was not alone. His wagon was loaded with five families and all their possessions. After a brief exchange of waves and nods, they continued on their way. No one felt much like talking.

The light of day was fading when they stopped to make camp. They were a solemn-looking group. It had been a long and frightening day for all of them.

Before they started out the next morning, Dr. Rose looked from one worried face to another and searched for words of encouragement. He finally cleared his throat and said, "Ladies, cheer up! Once we have crossed the bridge it will not take us long to reach the San Jacinto River. Today will be better, you will see."

Dilue believed him — at first.

When they came to Vince's Bridge, the wooden slats clattered noisily as the carts rolled across. Once they were over the bridge, Dilue looked around. The oak trees growing along the bayou draped with long strands of gray moss gave her the creeps. They moved slower and slower. Many people were clogging the road in front of them. Diluc was sure there must be 5,000 or more. They were all trying to get to the ferry at once. With the recent rains there was no way to cross the deep river but on the ferry. The people were pushing to get ahead, but they found they had to await their turn.

Finally, on the third day of waiting, the Rose party made it to the other side of the river. Dilue now counted fifty persons in their group. That included the Negroes from the Stafford wagon. A black man called Uncle Ned drove that big wagon. It was pulled by five yoke of oxen and a number of horses.

They were still twelve miles from the Trinity River when Dr. Rose learned it was on the rise. He ordered them to hurry along. Those on horseback rode on ahead. The carts moved slowly over the muddy road with its deep ruts and chug holes. The Stafford wagon was in the lead when it bogged into the mud and could not move. The carts tried to go around, but they too got stuck. Dilue's mother gathered some of the children into their cart while the others struggled to free the wagon. The children were hungry and thirsty, but they finally went to sleep when it grew dark. Dilue awoke the next morning to learn the wagons were still stuck. Margaret Rose walked with the children to a grove of trees some distance away. Once they were there, they met the ones who had ridden ahead. Dilue was disappointed to find that her father and Mr. Bundick had gone to the river to look for the ferry boat. It was hours later before the Stafford wagon and the carts were able to get out of the mud and catch up with them.

Dilue felt detached from the world around her. Numbed by hunger and fear, she thought of her brother and Uncle James. She knew her uncle was somewhere fighting Santa Anna's men, but where was Granville? Father had said they would meet once they crossed the first river. That had seemed ages ago. Had something happened to him? What else could happen?

It was well Dilue did not know.

Victory!

The horrors that followed were difficult for Dilue's eleven-year-old mind to comprehend. She sensed a feeling of urgency in the crowd. Word had come that Sam Houston's men were retreating from Santa Anna's men, and they were heading in their direction. Hundreds and hundreds of people clogged the road hoping to push ahead to cross over the rising waters of the Trinity River.

To make matters worse, many were sick. Some had measles, others whooping cough or sore throats. Margaret Rose was worried about her two-year-old. Missouri was feverish, but Father had no medicine to doctor her. There was nothing he could do.

Dilue could see the mob waiting on the bank long before their party reached the swollen river. The bewildered ferryman stared at the throng of people and shook his head.

"Listen to me," the boatman shouted. Everyone was silent. He went on. "Now, I know you all want to be first to get across but the only decent thing to do is let the sick ones go first. I'll come back with my ferry for the rest of you. So you with sick folk move up front. Now the rest just be patient, everyone will get to the other side."

A few grumbled but moved to one side. Father pushed ahead with his horse in order to clear the way for his family. With baby Elba clasped to her chest, Dilue was among the last aboard. Some 500 back on shore watched the boat glide into the swift current.

The ferryman spoke up again. "I could use some help. How about some of you giving me a hand? We'll make better time if you can clear the driftwood from the sides of the boat." Eight men volunteered for the job.

Dilue overheard someone moan, "Mother, do you think there are alligators in that water?"

Dilue shivered at the thought. No one answered the question.

In spite of the noise of the men moving the logs, Dilue heard a groan from Missy. Her eyes rolled, her body stiffened, jerked, then went limp. Mother was frantic. Father found Missy's lifeless hand to feel her pulse. After a few minutes he whispered hoarsely, "Margaret, I'm afraid her fever is up. Just hold her still." Mother scarcely moved. She felt so helpless watching the labored breathing of the two-year-old.

Mrs. Dyer reached over to pat Margaret's arm. "You had better take my horse. Missy is so sick. I can double up with someone."

"How kind of you, Sarah." Father was touched by their friend's kindness. He realized she could be endangering her own safety by being so generous. "Since Sarah's been good enough to lend us her horse, honey, you can take the girls and little Elba with you. I will take Missouri with me. Dilue, you had better carry my gun."

The swaying of the ferry changed as it slowed down. The ferryman shouted, "Everybody listen. When we come to a complete stop, you with horses move off first. The rest of you slide off easy like when it comes your turn. Now be careful — remember, no shoving or pushing. We don't want anyone hurt."

When the ferry stopped, Dilue peered into the shadows around them. She felt sure the man had made a terrible mistake. Even in the darkness, she could see there was water everywhere. One by one the people with horses rode off the side of the ferry. When it was Father's turn, he clasped Missouri tightly in one arm and the reins with the other. "Come on, Margaret," he shouted back over his shoulder.

With Ella seated in front of the saddle, and Dilue behind her, Margaret managed to keep up. It was not easy to hold onto the reins and Elba, too, but they made it without mishap. It was difficult to see the bridge for the water that covered it. The Roses had just crossed over when there was a terrible racket.

Someone screamed, "Look! The bridge broke in two and there's a man down there! I'm not sure he can swim. Someone throw him a rope."

It was a struggle, but they rescued the man and his cart. Dilue felt badly that his oxen drowned. She also felt sorry for the people with carts and wagons. With the bridge out, there was no way for them to get across the water-covered marsh. They were stranded in the muddy riverbottom with the water creeping into their carts. Dilue covered her ears with her hands trying to drown out their screams. They were begging for help, but there was little anyone could do until daylight.

Father led his family to higher ground and headed

for a fire he saw a short distance away in a grove of trees. When they neared the camp, a lady called to them. "Come on over and get something to eat." She looked from one to the other and decided Mother was the one who needed her help. "Here, hand me your girl while you get down. Then help yourself to supper — you look plumb tuckered out."

Truer words were never spoken. They were exhausted. It was good to be on solid ground near the warm fire. Dilue never knew she could be so hungry or that food could taste so good.

The woman cradled Missouri in her arms while they ate. "Now, when you're finished we'll find some dry clothes. Just look at you — you are all wet to the bone! There's enough sickness without you catchin' a death of cold in this night air. We may be kind of crowded, but the women and children can bed down in my wagon. And, Mister, you can sleep underneath. Won't be very comfortable, but it'll be dry." She peered down at Missy's whitish face and shook her head sadly. "Seems this little tyke is pretty sick. We'll do our best to make her comfortable, too."

Tears of appreciation rimmed Margaret's eyes. She was too weary to speak. Father had difficulty finding words with the lump in his throat. He could only mumble, "Thank you."

The next morning the men went back to the riverbottom to help the ones they had left behind. Although they were cold and hungry after a miserable night, they were overjoyed to see them. After much discussion, the men finally decided the only way to get them out of the marshes was to make a raft of logs. It was not easy, but they finished the crude raft. The men were able to move only a few people at a time without danger of it overturning. They found it slow work. In fact, it took four days to haul

54

everything out of the flooded riverbottom up to higher ground.

Once the group had things together again on the fifth day, they broke camp to head for the little town of Liberty. The man whose oxen had drowned sold his cart to Father for ten dollars. Now, at last, the Roses had a cart of their own.

The hardships they had been through were too much for little Missy. With each passing day she had grown weaker and weaker. They had just reached Liberty on the sixth morning when the child died quietly in her mother's arms. Margaret cried bitter tears of sorrow; she was undone by the loss. Everyone was so kind to her. The men helped Father bury little Missy in the cemetery. Someone quoted a scripture from the Bible from memory, and one of the women sang a song.

Everyone shared the sorrow of Missy's death, but the panic of war soon made the others return to concern about their own families. News came that Colonel Fannin and his men had been massacred at Goliad and that Santa Anna's army was only miles away. There were those who left, but Father decided Margaret was too weak and exhausted to travel any farther. A fellow named Martin told Father he was taking his family away from Liberty. He told Father he could use his house. That made Mother feel a little better.

By dark that night, everyone except the Roses and two other families had left the town. There was an uneasy silence in the air during the next day and the ones that followed. Dilue hid her fears by humming a song while she did what she could to help her mother. With the passing of time, the paleness left Margaret's cheeks, but she was still too weak to travel.

Father scouted around each morning to find something for them to eat. He never went far from the house. One day he returned with a yoke of oxen. He felt certain they belonged to the Staffords, but there was no sign of Adam or Granville. Father said the extra yoke of oxen could help pull their cart, but he was worried. Where could Granville be?

The temperatures of the April afternoons rose higher and higher during the next three weeks. The cabin was too warm for comfort. Outside under the trees a gentle breeze was usually blowing. It was there the family spent many hours.

Late one afternoon, Dilue asked her father what day it was. He rubbed his chin thoughtfully and said, "Today must be Thursday the twenty-first day of April. We left home five weeks ago today."

Dilue knew her mother must be thinking what she was. How could so many things happen in so short a time? They had not heard a word from Uncle James since he left to join General Houston. Where was he, and where was Granville?

They were each thinking their own thoughts when suddenly the silence was broken by a loud booming noise. "What's that? Thunder?"

Dilue's father glanced up at the sun-filled sky and shook his head. Before he could answer, there was another boom and another. He jumped to his feet shouting, "Cannons! I'd know that sound anywhere! And it is coming from the river — that's not far from here! We cannot stay here any longer. Dilue, you and Ella help your mother with little Elba while I yoke the oxen to the cart and get my horse. Now hurry!"

They wasted no time getting things together to be on their way again. The other two families were leaving, too. Father said there was safety in numbers and they should stay together.

It was pitch dark when they finally stopped to make camp for the night. They had just settled around the fire when Father heard something. "What's that?" he whispered loudly. "Listen!"

When they heard the sound of horse's hooves, the men grabbed their guns. A rider suddenly appeared in the distance from behind a grove of trees. He was waving his hat and yelling something, but he was too far away for them to make out his words until he rode nearer. "Stop!" he was shouting. "Turn back! It's over! The war is over!"

"What?"

"It's over! We've whipped the Mexicans! The war is over!"

Words tumbled out so rapidly it was difficult to understand the young man at first. "Yesterday — about four o'clock — near Lynchburg on the San Jacinto!"

"Lynchburg?" Father repeated. "Why, Lynchburg is less than fifteen miles from here!"

"That's right!"

"How long did the battle last?" one of the men asked.

"About twenty minutes — maybe less. And the last I heard, old Santa Anna hadn't been found. But, by now, I reckon our men have got him."

"What's your name, son?"

"McDermot — good old Irish name."

Father insisted Mr. McDermot eat supper and stay the night with them. He accepted gratefully; he said he had slept very little for weeks.

During the night, thunder and lightning rolled across the sky as rain began to fall. No one cared. Their dreams were of home.

Heading Home

The next morning after they said goodbye to Mr. McDermot, he rode off to spread the good news to everyone: the war was over! The Roses said farewells to the two families. They headed in opposite directions toward their homes.

In spite of the heavy rains the night before, the Roses crossed the Trinity River on the ferry without much delay. Crossing the swollen bayou was another matter. Father asked the ferryman about the best way to get across. The man said, "There is no bridge across the bayou. The only way to cross is go up to the mouth — that's about three miles from here. But be careful, Mister. There's alligators in that water. Quicksand, too!"

Dilue was glad the man did not say more. The rain and mud made that bayou frightening enough as it was. They made it to the other side without any problem. The only mishap was when Dilue's bonnet blew off into the swirling waters and was carried away. They watched it twirl round and round then vanish from sight. Dilue did not care about the hat, but Mother insisted she cover her head with an old cloth. She hated that.

It was late in the night when they found a place in Lynchburg to camp. The next morning they rode the ferry over the San Jacinto River to the battlefield. The odor of gunpowder still clung to the air. Dilue did not like the smell.

"Hello, folks," someone shouted. Dilue could scarcely believe her eyes. There stood their old neighbor, Leo Roark! At first everyone talked at once in their joy of seeing one another again. When Mother learned that Leo had been in the battle there at San Jacinto with General Houston, she asked about her brother, James Wells.

"James? Well, the last I saw of him he was riding with two other scouts to check on the Mexicans. Don't you worry, Mrs. Rose, I'm sure he will be all right. Say . . . would you like to walk over to see Santa Anna and the other prisoners? They are over yonder."

Margaret looked down at her tattered dress and shook her head. "No, Leo, after what we have been through I do not feel like seeing anyone. Besides, I am hardly dressed for visiting. Just look at me! I am wearing five weeks of mud. But the girls can go if they want to."

Dilue's hands flew to the cloth around her head. "Oh, Mother, I can't go anywhere looking like this! We might see someone I know! Leo, why don't we just look around here?"

They spent the next few hours on the San Jacinto battleground. Dilue thought she might faint when she accidentally stumbled over a body. She had seen few dead men before, and avoided looking at the face of the soldier.

59

The sight of dried blood on the ground beneath the Mexican made her weak.

Leo told of seeing General Houston's horse shot from under him just before a bullet pierced the general's leg. He asked Dilue if she would like to meet the man who had lead the Texans to victory. Leo said he was sitting under a tree not far from them. Dilue looked toward the tree. She said she really did not want to meet anyone looking the way she did, certainly not an important person like Gen. Sam Houston!

Once they toured the battlefield, Leo Roark rode with the Roses toward their home. The road was packed with weary travelers going in their direction. Dilue heard them talk of the towns that were now in ashes: San Felipe, Gonzales, Harrisburg, and many more. The Stafford sugarmill, blacksmith shop, and cotton gin had all been destroyed.

One of the men told Father that Adam Stafford had returned home sometime earlier. Dilue's mother asked, "And our son, Granville, do you have word of him?" She waited breathlessly for his answer.

"Granville? Why, he is fine! Did you hear our last shipment of cotton wasn't damaged but is waiting to be sold?"

Father was overjoyed with news of Granville and the cotton. He threw back his head and laughed for the first time in weeks. "You know the first thing I am gonna do when we sell that cotton? I'm buying a new bonnet for Dilue! Poor girl, she's wearing a rag tied around her head!"

Dilue's face turned as red as her hair, but even she had to chuckle about the rag. About that time two men rode into camp. No one paid much attention to them. When the taller one turned toward the fire, Mother gave a yell and threw her arms around the man's neck. She was crying something awful! Dilue had trouble recognizing Uncle James at first, for he had grown a bushy beard. What a joyous occasion that turned out to be for everyone.

The next morning they were up by dawn. With only miles to go, the Roses had only one thought — *home!* Just as Dilue was wondering if the house had burned to ashes or something, they rounded the bend in the road and there it stood — unharmed!

Dilue was certain that absolutely nothing could ever be more beautiful than that dear house. They soon discovered Santa Anna's men had torn out the floor looking for money and hidden treasure. Father's books and papers were scattered everywhere, but other than that, things were just the way they had left them.

Everyone was so busy poking through the rubble they did not hear Granville sneak up behind them until he yelled, "Welcome home!"

What a homecoming it was! Dilue felt she might explode with joy. The war was over, Texas had won her independence, and Dilue — the Texas Rose — was home once more.

Epilogue

In the years that followed the Texas Revolution, there were many changes in Dilue Rose's life. Her father died in 1839 from yellow fever. That same year, before her fourteenth birthday, Dilue married Ira Harris.

Dilue and her husband had nine children. Before her death in 1914, at the age of eighty-nine, Dilue wrote of her childhood experiences in early Texas. Her stories were so vivid and complete they have been retold in a number of history books. *The Quarterly of the Texas State Historical Association* printed "The Reminiscences of Mrs. Dilue Harris" in the early 1900s.

Bibliography

Books

Crawford, Ann Fears, and Crystal S. Ragsdale. *Women in Texas*. Austin: Eakin Press, 1982.

Harris, Dilue (Rose). *Life in Early Texas, The Reminiscences of Dilue Harris*. Richmond, Texas: Price & Price Publications. Reprint of *Quarterly of the Texas State Historical Association*, Vol. 4, No. 3 (January 1901).

Hiatt, Dean B. *Mid Muddle and Mud*. Austin: Nortex Press, 1980.

Pool, William. *Texas Wilderness to Space Age*. San Antonio: Naylor, 1962.

Reese, James V., and Lorrin Kennamer. *Texas, Land of Contrast*. Austin: Benson Company, 1978.

Richard, J. A., and Clyde Inez Martin. *Under Texas Skies*. Austin: Benson Company, 1964.

Webb, Walter Prescott. Ed. *The Handbook of Texas*. Vol. 1. Austin: Texas State Historical Association, 1952.

Periodicals

Harris, Dilue Rose. "The Reminiscences of Mrs. Dilue Harris." *The Quarterly of the Texas State Historical Association,* October 1900, January 1901, January 1904.

ABOUT THE AUTHOR

Rita Kerr taught in San Antonio elementary schools for twenty-seven years before retiring four years ago to devote her time to writing. A native of Oklahoma, she was born in Okmulgee and moved to Texas as a teenager. She attended San Antonio College and received her bachelor of arts degree from Trinity University. She is married and has two children.

Today she spends much of her time presenting programs on Texas history to school children. She is author of *Girl of the Alamo* and appears in costume as Susanna Dickinson in her school programs.